WALT DISNEY PICTURES
PRESENTS
THE RESCUERS
DOWN UNDER

LONGMEADOW
PRESS

Twin Books

One morning, as the sun rose over the Australian outback, a young boy named Cody raced to the sound of an urgent alarm. As he ran through the forest, weaving through trees and jumping over rocks, he wondered who was in trouble.

Finally, in a forest clearing, Cody found his kangaroo friend, Faloo, who had sounded the call for help.

"Who was caught?" Cody asked his friend.

"Marahute, the great golden eagle," replied Faloo. "She's trapped high on a cliff in a poacher's net. You're the only one who can reach her."

Cody climbed on the kangaroo's back, and the two of them raced through the forest.

Soon Cody and Faloo arrived at a tall cliff. Faloo pointed to the top. "Marahute's up on that ridge. Be careful, little friend."

"No worries. I can do it," said Cody, as he began climbing the sheer rock face.

When Cody reached the top, he peered over the edge.
Before him, trapped in a net, was the enormous eagle.

Marahute screeched in fright.

"I'm not going to hurt you," Cody assured her. "I'm here to
help."

Cody took out a pocketknife and began cutting through the
ropes. Before he could finish, Maranute spread her
magnificent wings and burst free.

The force of the eagle's wings sent Cody reeling backward over the cliff. Just as he was about to hit the ground, Marahute flew beneath him and lifted him into the sky on her back.

Together, they soared past the cliff, up into the heavy
clouds. "Higher! Higher!" Cody yelled with joy. Then he held
on tight as Marahute turned and dove toward a shimmering
river.

After skimming the water's surface, they climbed back into
the sky.

Marahute took Cody to her secret nest atop the cliff. The boy peered inside and gently touched the eggs.

"Are they going to hatch soon?" asked Cody.

Marahute nodded yes, and as a gift, she gave him one of her beautiful golden feathers.

The eagle returned Cody to the forest, and the boy headed home, pretending to glide like an airplane.

On the way, Cody discovered a mouse caught in a tiny trap. He knelt down to set it free.

"Get away!" cried the mouse. "It's a trap! It's a big trap!"

The ground gave way beneath them, and they both tumbled into a pit.

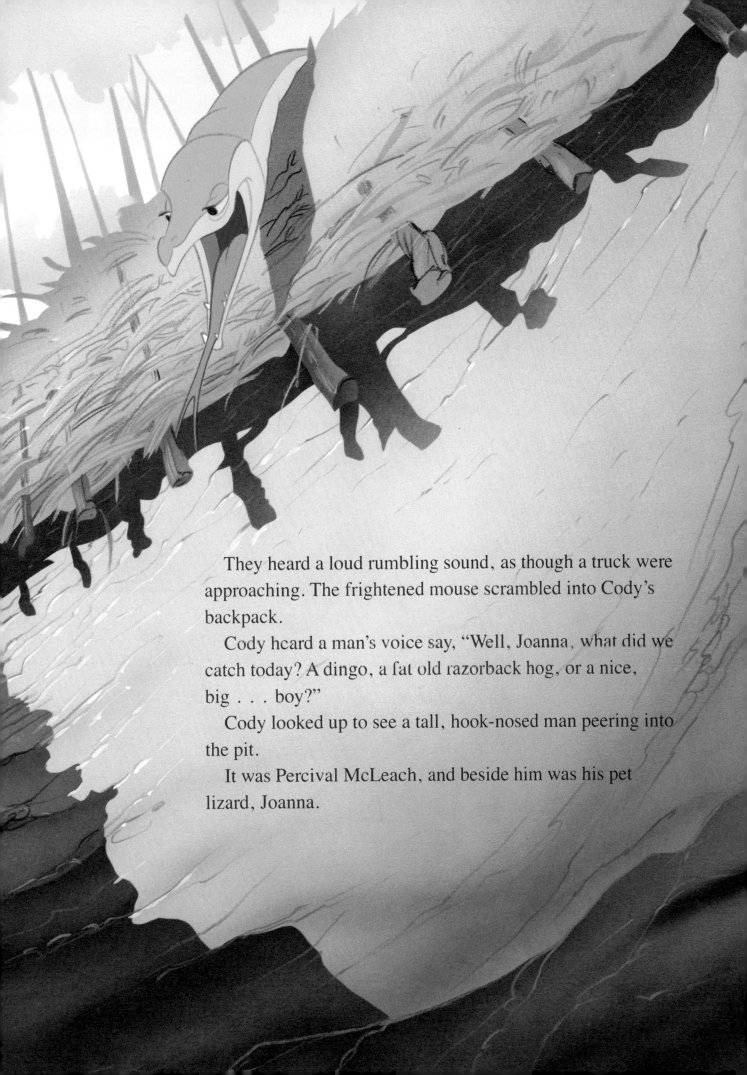

They heard a loud rumbling sound, as though a truck were approaching. The frightened mouse scrambled into Cody's backpack.

Cody heard a man's voice say, "Well, Joanna, what did we catch today? A dingo, a fat old razorback hog, or a nice, big . . . boy?"

Cody looked up to see a tall, hook-nosed man peering into the pit.

It was Percival McLeach, and beside him was his pet lizard, Joanna.

When McLeach saw Cody in the pit, he blamed Joanna for digging the hole. "My dumb lizard's always trying to bury squirrels out here," he explained.

"That's not true!" cried Cody. "This is a poacher's trap, and capturing wild animals is against the law!"

"Trap?" asked McLeach. "What makes you think that, boy? You've been down in that lizard hole too long. C'mon, I'll help you out."

McLeach lifted Cody out of the pit. When the boy turned around, the poacher saw Marahute's feather tied to Cody's backpack.

"Say, who gave you that pretty feather, boy?" asked McLeach.

"It's a secret," answered Cody, afraid that McLeach would try to recapture the eagle. "It was a present from a friend."

McLeach glared at him. "Now you just tell me where I can find the mama eagle and her eggs."

"No, I won't!" cried Cody. He slipped out of his backpack and broke into a run.

While the poacher raced after Cody, the mouse scurried out of the backpack and into the brush.

From his hiding place, the mouse watched McLeach grab
Cody and stuff him into the Bushwhacker—the big poaching
truck in which McLeach kept captured animals.

After the truck roared off, the mouse sped away to
telegraph the Rescue Aid Society: an organization of mice
dedicated to rescuing prisoners like Cody.

As the message was being relayed, the top two R.A.S. agents were dining at a fancy mouse restaurant in the same building as the society's headquarters. The restaurant was located on top of a chandelier in a larger restaurant, and it was just as splendid as the people place below.

During the meal, Bernard had been trying his best to propose marriage to his companion, Bianca.

After dinner, Bernard reached into his pocket and clutched an engagement ring. "Miss Bianca, I was wondering . . ."

"Yes, Bernard?" she asked, smiling.

"Miss Bianca, would you . . ." Bernard continued. But before he could finish, the ring slipped through a hole in his pocket and a waiter kicked it under the table!

Excusing himself, Bernard dove after the ring.

As Bernard crawled across the floor in search of the ring, Miss Bianca received news of the kidnapping from the headwaiter, Francois.

"Oh, the poor boy!" exclaimed Miss Bianca. "This is dreadful. I must tell Bernard, so we can leave for Australia immediately!"

Miss Bianca didn't know it, but at that very moment Bernard was trying to remove the ring from a rich old lady's toe, where it had become wedged after rolling across the floor.

With much effort, Bernard popped the ring off the dowager's toe before she knew what was happening. Then he zipped out from under the table and hurried back to Miss Bianca.

Bianca spoke first. "Francois told me all about it. I think it's a marvelous idea."

"You do?" exclaimed Bernard, happily surprised that Miss Bianca would marry him. "How does next April sound to you?"

"Heavens, no. We must act immediately. Tonight!"

Without delay, Bianca dragged Bernard to R.A.S. headquarters. There he learned that what she had agreed to was a rescue mission—not a wedding!

That night, in the middle of a
violent snowstorm, Bernard
and Bianca located Albatross
Airlines and its new manager,
Wilbur.

The large bird was so busy
singing and dancing away to a
loud rock 'n' roll song that
Bernard had trouble getting his
attention.

"I beg your pardon, but we
need to . . ." attempted
Bernard. "Excuse me, if I could
just have one minute . . ." he
tried again. Finally, he yelled,
"Hey!" and snapped off the
tape player.

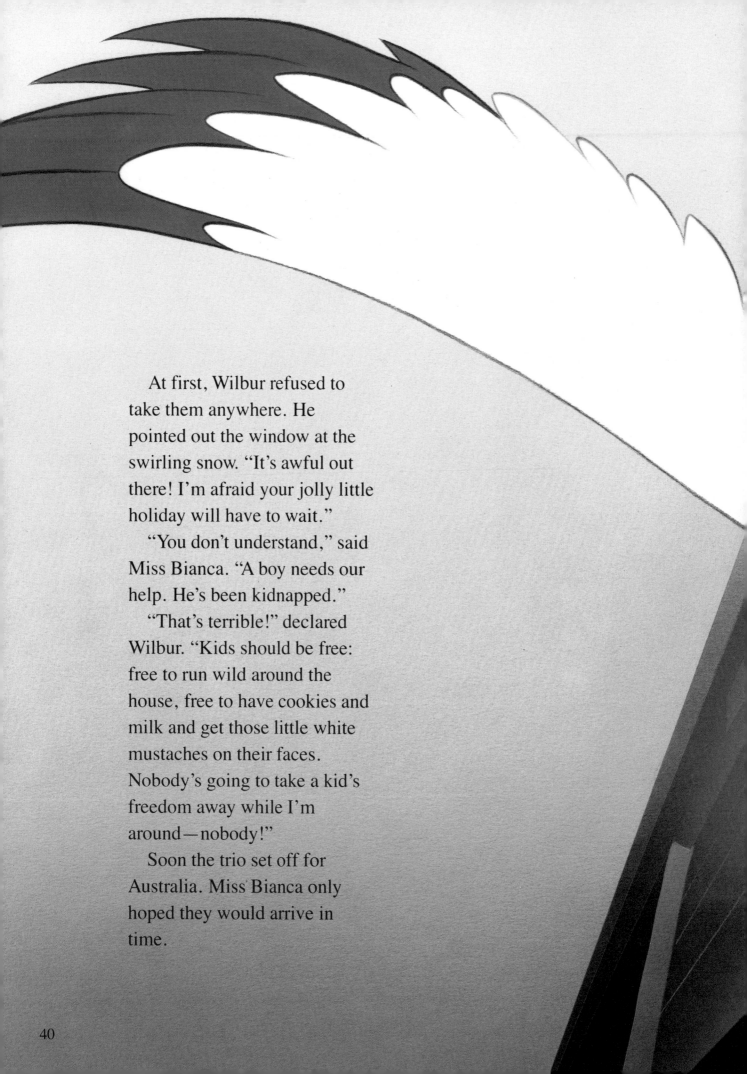

At first, Wilbur refused to take them anywhere. He pointed out the window at the swirling snow. "It's awful out there! I'm afraid your jolly little holiday will have to wait."

"You don't understand," said Miss Bianca. "A boy needs our help. He's been kidnapped."

"That's terrible!" declared Wilbur. "Kids should be free: free to run wild around the house, free to have cookies and milk and get those little white mustaches on their faces. Nobody's going to take a kid's freedom away while I'm around—nobody!"

Soon the trio set off for Australia. Miss Bianca only hoped they would arrive in time.

They made it safely across the ocean, then headed for the outback. When Wilbur reached Mugwomp Flats, he used a speaker box to alert the control tower.

Jake, the kangaroo-mouse flight controller, replied, "Negative! You'll have to turn back. Our runway isn't long enough for a bird your size."

"Look, pal," snorted the albatross, "I can land this thing on a dime."

A dime*store* would be more like it. Wilbur bounced, skidded, and crashed to a halt.

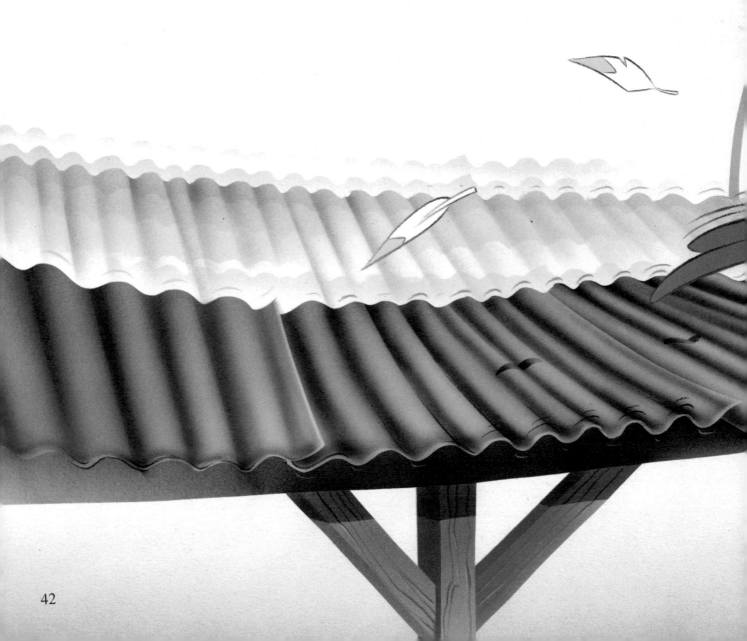

The albatross had even more trouble with the luggage than with the landing.

He let his passengers out of the sardine-tin cabin, then bent down to pick up their bags. "Ah, oh! My back!" he yelled. "Big-time hurt!"

Wilbur would have to stay in the hospital, while Bernard and Bianca went on without him.

Outside the hospital, Jake asked Miss Bianca if she and Bernard were going to rescue the boy whom McLeach had kidnapped.

"Why, that's right. How did you know?"

"It's hard to keep secrets in the outback, Miss," he replied. "So which way are you taking? The Suicide Trail through Nightmare Canyon, or the shortcut at Satan's Ridge?"

"Wait a minute!" cried Bernard. "I don't see any of those places on the map!"

Jake laughed. "A map's no good in the outback. What you really need is someone who knows the territory."

After Jake agreed to be their guide, Miss Bianca stared at the bleak landscape before them. "How long will it take us to get to McLeach's?" she asked.

"When you travel outback-style," answered Jake, "not long at all."

Within seconds, they were boarding a sugar glider—an Australian flying squirrel.

Miss Bianca found a seat
next to Jake on the squirrel's
back, while Bernard held onto
its tail. Jake turned around and
eyed Bernard. "All set there,
Berno?"

"All set," replied Bernard.
The sugar glider took off,
and they sailed over the dry
Australian landscape. Bernard
had just begun to feel
comfortable when he found
himself tossed into the bushes
as the sugar glider landed.

They had reached Nightmare Canyon, and Jake went to scout up more transportation. While he was gone, Bernard got up his nerve again. Fingering the engagement ring tucked inside his pocket, he cleared his throat.

"Uh, Miss Bianca," he began, "now that we're alone, I've been wanting to ask you something."

"Yes, what is it?" asked Miss Bianca.

"Well, um . . . it's like this. I would be honored if you—"

"Look out." shouted Jake, pushing Bernard into the river.

When Bernard surfaced, he saw Jake staring a giant python in the eye. "Now, look," he snarled to the snake, "we've got a long way to go. You're going to take us there, and you're not going to give me any trouble about it, right?"

The python nodded, and the riders took their places.

Miss Bianca was impressed with Jake's skill and daring. Bernard was not!

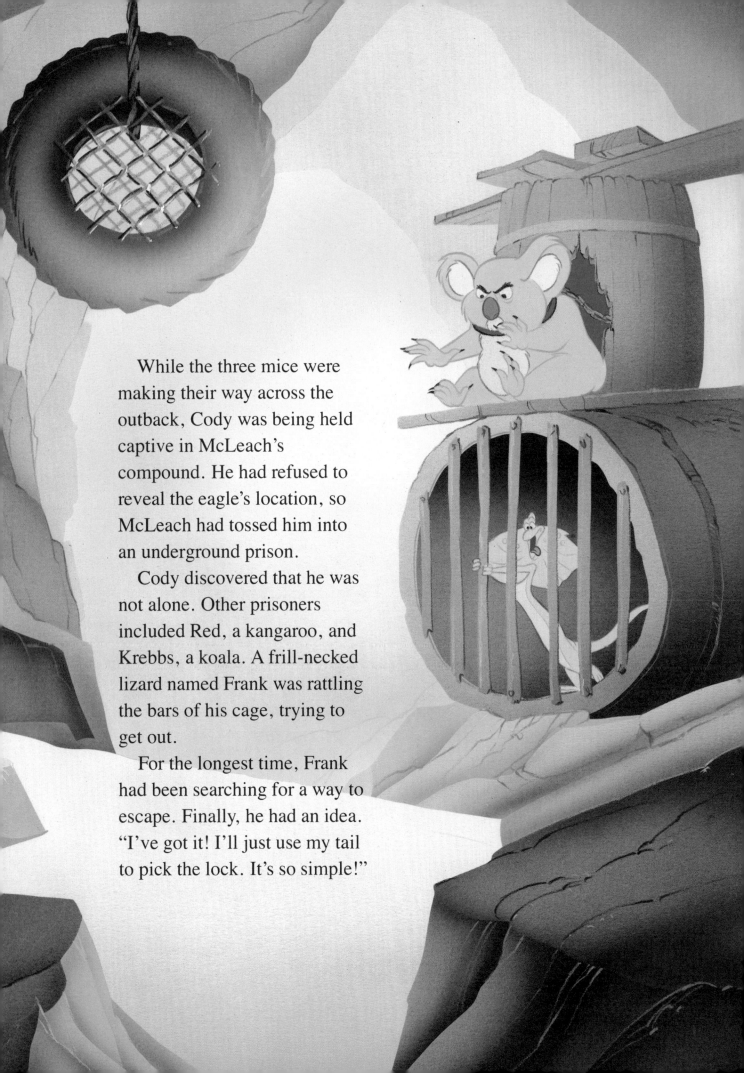

While the three mice were making their way across the outback, Cody was being held captive in McLeach's compound. He had refused to reveal the eagle's location, so McLeach had tossed him into an underground prison.

Cody discovered that he was not alone. Other prisoners included Red, a kangaroo, and Krebbs, a koala. A frill-necked lizard named Frank was rattling the bars of his cage, trying to get out.

For the longest time, Frank had been searching for a way to escape. Finally, he had an idea. "I've got it! I'll just use my tail to pick the lock. It's so simple!"

And it *was* simple. Frank managed to open his cage. "I'm free!" he shouted, jumping up and down. "Free, free, free!"

Krebbs eyed the lizard and said, "Double or nothing, he's caught in five minutes."

Cody blurted, "Go get the keys, Frank!"

The frill-necked lizard calmed down long enough to get the keys off a hook. But as he tiptoed past the door, he dropped them with a loud crash.

Joanna burst through the door and headed straight for Frank.

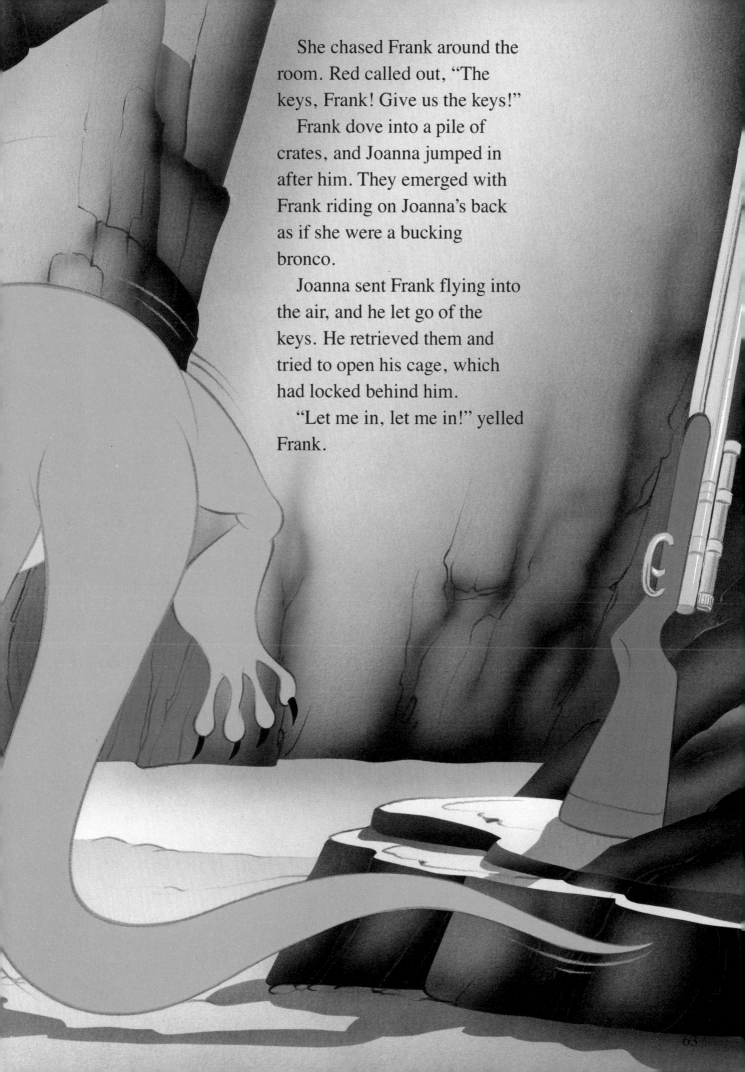

She chased Frank around the room. Red called out, "The keys, Frank! Give us the keys!"

Frank dove into a pile of crates, and Joanna jumped in after him. They emerged with Frank riding on Joanna's back as if she were a bucking bronco.

Joanna sent Frank flying into the air, and he let go of the keys. He retrieved them and tried to open his cage, which had locked behind him.

"Let me in, let me in!" yelled Frank.

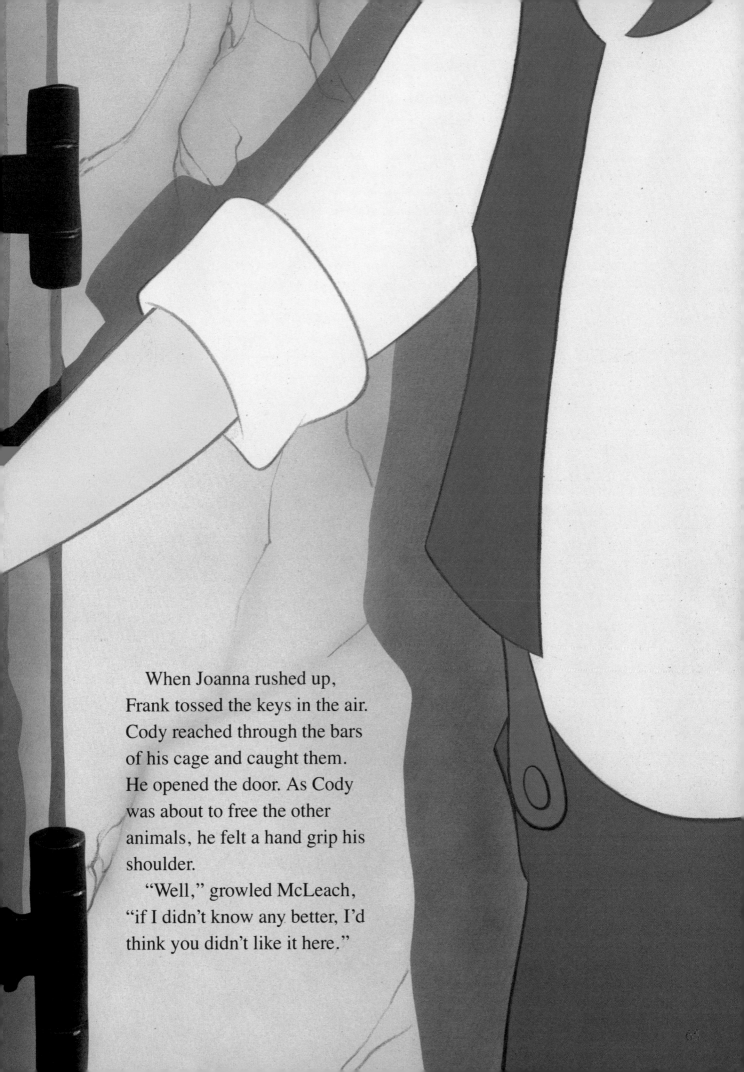

When Joanna rushed up,
Frank tossed the keys in the air.
Cody reached through the bars
of his cage and caught them.
He opened the door. As Cody
was about to free the other
animals, he felt a hand grip his
shoulder.

"Well," growled McLeach,
"if I didn't know any better, I'd
think you didn't like it here."

67

In the meantime, Jake and the Rescuers continued their journey through the outback. Without stopping to rest, they flew through the night on the backs of fireflies.

The next morning, they arrived at McLeach's compound.
Bianca stared at the huge steel door. "There's no time to
waste," she said. "We must try to get in."

Jake said jokingly, "Has anyone considered trying 'Open, sesame'?"

To his astonishment, the bottom of the door rose and the mice were scooped up on top of it. They peeked over the edge and saw McLeach shove Cody out of the compound.

"It's all over, boy!" McLeach yelled after Cody. "Your bird's dead! Somebody shot her!"

"No! It's not true!" the boy cried.

"Well, it is! You'd better get out of here before I change my mind. Go on, get!" McLeach grinned, then added, "Too bad about the eagle's eggs, eh? They'll never survive without their mother."

Shocked, Cody ran off into the outback, unaware that the mice had been watching him. McLeach was watching too, an evil smile on his face.

From the top of the door, Bernard asked, "Why is he letting the boy go?"

"It must be a trick!" exclaimed Jake.

They heard an engine kick into life. Within seconds, the Bushwhacker emerged with McLeach in the driver's seat. Beside him sat Joanna.

"I don't know what he's up to," said Jake, "but we can't let him get away. Hurry, jump onto the truck!"

In the Bushwhacker, McLeach followed Cody to the cliff. Jake and the Rescuers saw Cody climb to the eagle's nest, and they hurried after him.

"Who are you?" Cody asked when he saw the mice.

"There's no time to explain," cried Miss Bianca. "You're in great danger!"

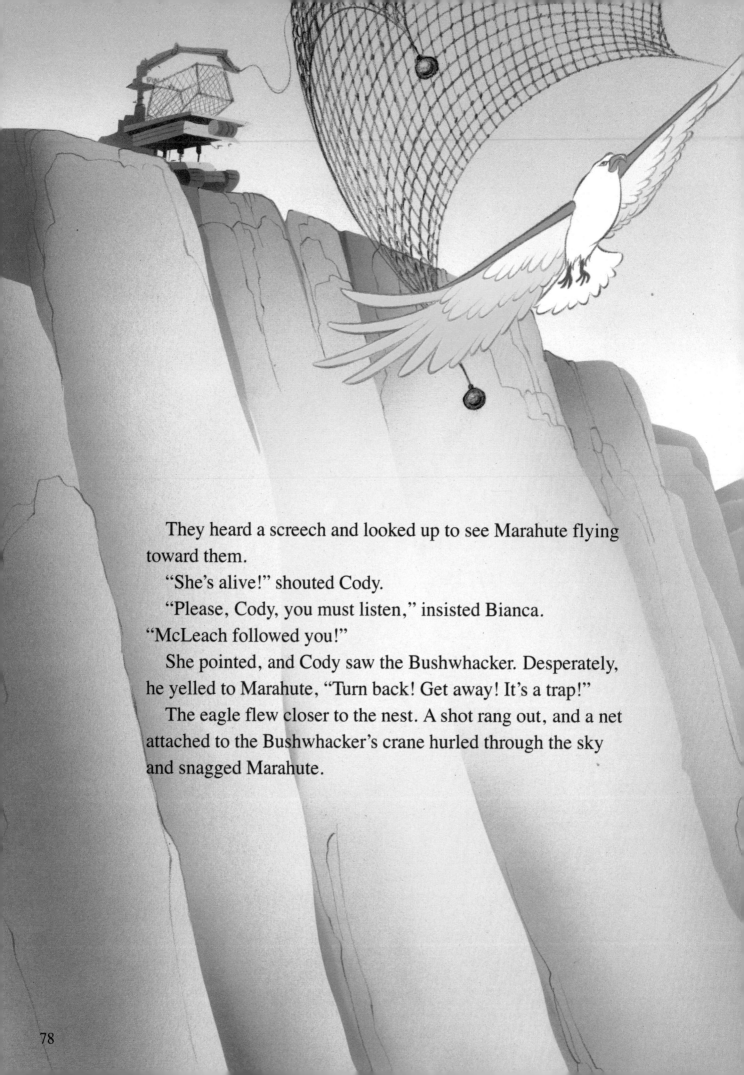

They heard a screech and looked up to see Marahute flying toward them.

"She's alive!" shouted Cody.

"Please, Cody, you must listen," insisted Bianca. "McLeach followed you!"

She pointed, and Cody saw the Bushwhacker. Desperately, he yelled to Marahute, "Turn back! Get away! It's a trap!"

The eagle flew closer to the nest. A shot rang out, and a net attached to the Bushwhacker's crane hurled through the sky and snagged Marahute.

Horrified, Cody watched as the net swung from the crane. He leaped from the cliff and grabbed hold of the bundle.

Thinking quickly, Jake lassoed Cody's ankle with his rope and handed the other end to the Rescuers. "Hold on tight, you two," he said. "We're going for a ride."

Bianca managed to grab the rope, but Bernard missed it. "Bernard!" cried Bianca, as the net was raised by the crane, leaving Bernard behind.

The net reached the top of the cliff, and McLeach dumped his prisoners into the Bushwhacker cage.

The poacher grinned and said to his pet lizard, "Just look at that eagle, Joanna—the rarest bird in the world. It's going to make me rich. And you can make sure that the bird stays rare. How about some great big eagle eggs for supper?"

The poacher tied a harness to Joanna, then pushed her over the edge of the cliff.

At the nest, the lizard bit into one egg after another. Ugh! They were hard as rocks. She tossed the eggs over the cliff and tugged on the rope so McLeach would lift her.

84

As soon as the lizard was gone, Bernard emerged from under the nest. "Okay, you guys," he said to the eggs, which he had hidden. "She fell for it."

Just then, something tumbled into the nest. "Wilbur!" cried Bernard.

"Ahhhh!" Wilbur was just as surprised to see Bernard as the mouse was to see him. The albatross had just made a daring escape from the hospital.

Bernard tried to convince Wilbur to sit on the eggs until Marahute could be rescued. Wilbur resisted. "Don't look at me like that, Bernard. I will never, ever sit on those eggs."

But pretty soon Wilbur was perched uncomfortably on the eggs while Bernard hurried after the Bushwhacker.

McLeach drove his poaching truck straight to Croc Falls. He tied up Cody and used the crane to dangle his prisoner over the river. On the opposite shore, crocodiles slithered into the water.

The crane lowered Cody, and he kicked at the snapping reptiles. From the truck, Marahute screeched while Bianca murmured, "Oh, Bernard, please hurry."

As Cody was about to become the crocodiles' dinner, the Bushwhacker's engine went dead.

Bianca saw Bernard dash out from under the cab with the keys in his hand. "You see," she cried to Jake, "he did make it!"

Joanna noticed Bernard and raced toward him. He threw the keys to Jake and Bianca, then darted away.

As the big lizard pursued Bernard, McLeach began shooting at the rope holding Cody.

Bernard sprinted toward McLeach. He ran between the poacher's legs, and Joanna crashed into her master. The three of them tumbled into the river. At the same moment, the rope snapped and Cody fell.

They all struggled in the water, Joanna fought her way to shore and waved good-bye as McLeach was pulled downstream. The crocodiles rushed toward him, but they lost him to the thundering falls.

Meanwhile, Bernard and Cody battled the current. They fought harder and harder as the current dragged them toward the falls. Finally, they plunged over the edge.

The swirling water turned to rushing air, as they felt themselves being lifted into the sky. Marahute had caught them in her talons! On her back rode Jake and Bianca.

They soared into the clouds: Marahute, Cody, Jake, and the two courageous mice from the Rescue Aid Society—the charming Miss Bianca, and the dauntless Bernard, who had saved the day by running off with the keys.

Bolstered by the successful rescue, Bernard was finally able to ask Miss Bianca to marry him. And marry him she did.

This edition produced for
Longmeadow Press
by Twin Books Corp

ISBN 0-681-41430-8

Printed in Hong Kong